Elementary

Classes Are CANCELED!

By Jack Chabert
Illustrated by Matt Loveridge,
based on the art of Sam Ricks

BRANCHES™
SCHOLASTIC INC.

READ ALL THE Eerie Elementary ADVENTURES!

1

2

3

4

5

6

7

8

MORE BOOKS

COMING SOON!

Table of Contents

To Blastie — JC

Library of Congress Cataloging-in-Publication Data

Names: Chabert, Jack, author. | Chabert, Jack. Eerie Elementary ; 7.
Title: Classes are CANCELED! / by Jack Chabert.
Description: New York, NY : Branches/Scholastic Inc., [2017] | Series: Eerie Elementary ; 7 | Summary: Eerie Elementary seems to be falling down around the students and teachers, so Principal Winik decides the school must be torn down, but Sam, Lucy, and Antonio suspect that somehow this is all part of Orson Eerie's evil plan to live forever—and if it is they must find a way to prevent the demolition.

ISBN 978-93-5275-299-7

Subjects: LCSH: Haunted schools—Juvenile fiction. | Elementary schools—Juvenile fiction. | Scientists—Juvenile fiction. | Building—Design and construction—Juvenile fiction. | Horror tales. | CYAC: Horror stories. | Haunted places—Fiction. | Schools—Fiction. | Scientists—Fiction. | Buildings—Fiction.
Classification: LCC PZ7.C3313 Cl 2017 | DDC 813.6 [Fic] —dc23 LC record available at https://lccn.loc.gov/2017015798

First edition, December 2017
Illustrated by Matt Loveridge
Edited by Katie Carella
Book design by Maria Mercado

This reprint edition: February 2024

Printed in India

PLAQUE ATTACK!

1

"Everyone, please line up!" Sam Graves shouted.

"No running!" Lucy yelled.

"No pushing either!" Antonio added.

It was morning outside Eerie Elementary. Sam and his best friends were standing on the front steps — on hall monitor duty. They were making sure everyone lined up in an orderly fashion.

"Do you think our classmates think we're annoying?" Antonio asked.

"They better not think we're annoying!" Lucy exclaimed. "Not after everything we've done for them!"

It was true. Sam, Antonio, and Lucy had done *a lot*. At Eerie Elementary, hall monitors were *different*. They did more than just patrol the halls. It was their job to protect everyone. The hall monitors were the only students who knew the truth . . .

Eerie Elementary was alive! It was a living, breathing thing that fed on students. A mad scientist named Orson Eerie designed the school. He had found a way to live forever — he became the school. Orson Eerie was the school, and the school was Orson Eerie!

Eerie Elementary was almost one hundred years old. A stone plaque hung high above the front steps. There was a date on the plaque. 1923: the year the school had been built.

Students stood lined up around the steps. They were waiting for the doors to open so school could begin.

Sam gazed up at the plaque.

A twisted and tangled feeling suddenly spread inside Sam's gut. As hall monitor, Sam could sense things that other students couldn't. He could *feel* when something was wrong. Right now, Sam had that feeling.

Just then, small bits of stone fluttered down, like winter snow. Sam watched as a thin crack sliced across the plaque . . .

JUST THE BEGINNING

2

The plaque hung at a crooked angle. It was about to fall!

Sam's heart was pounding. "Watch out!" he shouted.

Antonio and Lucy spun around. "What is it?" Lucy asked.

"The plaque —" Sam began to say. Antonio and Lucy looked up. They could see the heavy stone would fall in seconds!

"Everyone! Off the steps! Quickly!" the three friends shouted.

Students and teachers ran. No one knew what was happening — they just knew the hall monitors said to MOVE!

Sam watched the plaque tumble from its place above the door. It seemed to happen in slow motion — like a scene from a movie.

He dove out of the way!

The plaque shattered against the steps.

A wrinkled hand reached out to help Sam. Sam looked up and saw Mr. Nekobi, the old man who took care of the school. Mr. Nekobi had chosen Sam to be hall monitor. He had told Sam the terrible truth about Eerie Elementary! It was a secret Mr. Nekobi had only shared with Sam, Antonio, and Lucy.

Principal Winik burst out the front doors. "Is everyone safe?" he asked. He looked very worried.

Sam nodded. “Everyone’s okay.”

Students were standing up and brushing themselves off. No one was badly hurt.

“This is not good,” Principal Winik said nervously.

“I’ll get these front steps cleaned up,” Mr. Nekobi said.

“Enough milling around!” Ms. Grinker barked. Ms. Grinker was Sam, Antonio, and Lucy’s third-grade teacher. She shuffled her students into the building.

Sam, Lucy, and Antonio helped students step over the broken plaque.

"The school day just started and Orson is already up to no good!" Antonio said.

"Maybe Orson had nothing to do with this," Lucy said. "The school is old. Maybe the plaque fell on its own."

"Possibly . . . ," Sam said. He eyed the strange, monstrous school. It was just a building — but it looked *tired*. It looked more run-down than usual.

Orson Eerie is planning something big, Sam thought, *and that falling plaque was just the beginning . . .*

A DANGEROUS DAY

3

Sam, Antonio, and Lucy could not stop thinking about the close call on the steps, but their classmates were already focused on something else. There was an exciting new addition to their classroom.

A small cage sat on Ms. Grinker's desk. Inside was a very furry and very adorable hamster. Students gathered around to get a look.

"She's soooo cute!" one student burst out.

"This is Squeakers," Ms. Grinker said. It was Ms. Grinker's first day back. "I heard you were good while I was gone. So I brought Squeakers in as a surprise."

Sam glanced at Lucy and Antonio. Ms. Grinker's week away from school had been *weird*. They had had a strange substitute — Jasper Eerie, the great-great-grandson of evil Orson Eerie. Jasper even lived in Orson Eerie's old house! But it turned out he only wanted to help Sam and his friends.

Every student in class got a moment to play with Squeakers. The hamster was so cute that even Sam began to forget about the falling plaque.

But then —

AIIIIEEEE!!!

Hot steam was blasting from the radiator!

"Oh my!" Ms. Grinker exclaimed. She raced to turn it off. And she looked relieved when the bell rang for lunch.

"First, the plaque fell, and then the radiator broke," Lucy said as the friends walked down the hall. "This day is weird."

There was a lot of chatter throughout the lunchroom. Almost every student had heard about some near-disaster! There were tales of the school stage crumbling, ceilings cracking, and floorboards busting.

"Dangerous stuff is happening all over school!" Antonio said as he bit into one of his famous peanut butter and jelly sandwiches.

At recess, Sam and his friends learned that the school nurse had been *very* busy that morning. A broken water fountain had squashed a student's foot. Another student twisted her ankle dodging a falling pipe.

RING!

Recess was over. Sam and his friends walked to their next class: gym.

The hallway looked different . . .

"There are new cracks in the floors," Lucy said.

"Lockers are hanging off their hinges," Antonio added.

"*Everything* looks run-down," Sam said. "It is *not normal* for a building to suddenly just fall apart!"

Sam had a tight feeling in his gut. It was the same feeling he had gotten before the plaque fell. It was the same feeling Sam *always* got when the school was about to strike!

He stepped inside the gym.

GYM CLASS CHAOS!

4

Sam felt a trembling beneath his feet. Small cracks were forming across the shiny wooden gym floor. He looked up and saw the ceiling splitting apart! Sam turned to warn Lucy and Antonio — but they had already started running across the gym!

"It's Dodgeball Day!" Lucy called over her shoulder as she raced toward the gym closet.

“My favorite!” Antonio said as he sped after her.

The gym teacher, Mr. Kirkpatrick, was pulling out a cart of dodgeballs.

Sam felt the cracks in the floor growing larger. He thought, *I need to get Lucy and Antonio’s attention!*

Mr. Kirkpatrick rolled dodgeballs across the floor. Soon, brightly colored balls were everywhere.

“Mr. Kirkpatrick!” Sam yelled. He darted around the bouncing balls and slid to a stop in front of his teacher. “You *have* to cancel class today!”

"Sam Graves," Mr. Kirkpatrick said. His hands were curled into fists that rested on his waist. "You need to toughen up. No one is getting out of Dodgeball Day!"

Sam groaned. "It's not that," he started to say, but then —

"OOF!"

Sam wheezed as a ball slammed into his stomach. He tumbled onto his butt.

Sam gasped. It was like the floor was made of thin ice. The cracks beneath him grew and splintered. Sam scrambled to his feet.

Mr. Kirkpatrick split the class into two teams. The game was about to start.

Sam spotted Antonio and Lucy. He began hurrying toward them, but a piercing whistle sliced through the air.

"BEGIN!" Mr. Kirkpatrick shouted.

"Argh!" Sam exclaimed as balls pounded him from left and right. He finally reached Antonio and Lucy.

"Why aren't you playing?" Lucy asked.

"Listen," Sam said. "Something bad is about to happen —"

Before Sam could finish, something bad *did* happen.

The floor was splitting apart and ceiling tiles started raining down! Sam's classmates cried out.

"Everyone! Follow me!" Sam shouted. "We have to get out of here!"

Frightened classmates looked to Sam. Even Mr. Kirkpatrick seemed terrified.

KRACKA-SLAM!

A huge chunk of ceiling crashed to the floor and blocked the exit. Everyone was trapped inside the crumbling, collapsing gymnasium.

DODGEBALL DISASTER!

5

Sam stared at the exit. *Rubble is blocking the doors!* he thought.

A basketball hoop toppled and smashed against the floorboards. Sam's classmates all huddled together at the center of the gym.

"What do we do?" Lucy asked.

"We need to get everyone out of here!" Antonio exclaimed.

"We have to clear away the rubble to get out the doors!" Sam said.

Then —

SNAP! SNAP!

Sam looked up. Dozens of lights dotted the high ceiling. One was plummeting toward them!

"Watch out!" Antonio said.

Lucy didn't have time to get out of the way. Instead, she lifted a dodgeball over her head. The light slammed into the ball and bounced off. It shattered against the floor.

"Good thinking, Lucy!" Sam said. He turned to his classmates. "Hold up your dodgeballs! Use them like shields!"

"Do what he says!" Mr. Kirkpatrick said. Sam saw his gym teacher hunched beneath the bleachers.

"Lucy! Antonio! Come with me!" Sam said. He lifted his dodgeball and they raced toward the doors.

The lamps bounced off and spun through the air. Floorboards burst open as Sam, Lucy, and Antonio sped across the gym.

At last, they reached the pile of rubble. Sam grabbed the wreckage and pulled at it. Lucy and Antonio dragged debris away from the doors.

They finally cleared the way. Sam pushed the doors — but they wouldn't open!

"They're locked!" Sam said.

Sam turned around. He saw his classmates holding dodgeballs above their heads.

"What if . . . ," Antonio started.

"We use the dodgeballs . . . ," Lucy went on.

"To open the doors!" Sam exclaimed.

Antonio cupped his hands over his mouth and shouted, "Listen, everyone! Throw your dodgeballs at the doors!"

But their classmates didn't move.

"Throw the balls now!" Mr. Kirkpatrick barked.

Their teacher's voice forced the students to act. Twenty-one dodgeballs flew screaming toward the doors . . .

SCHOOL'S OUT

6

KA-BOOM!

Every dodgeball slammed into the doors.

The doors flung open. The students sped into the hall.

The entire school seemed to be waiting there. Principal Winik stood alongside Ms. Grinker and Mr. Nekobi.

"Why were these doors locked?" Principal Winik barked.

Sam looked to Antonio and Lucy. They knew it was the school *itself* that had locked the doors. And it was the school *itself* that had caused the gymnasium to fall apart.

"As of now, the gym is off-limits!" Principal Winik announced.

Sam eyed Mr. Nekobi. They both understood that this was not about the gym — it was about the *school.*

"Principal Winik," Mr. Nekobi said, "many things have gone wrong today: the stone plaque fell, a toilet exploded, a heater burst, and now *this.*"

"You're right," the principal replied. "We can't have students in danger. I'm canceling school for the rest of the day."

Sam was desperate to discuss the day's events with Mr. Nekobi, but there was no chance to talk. Ms. Grinker led the class outside.

Sam's classmates were thrilled to be leaving early. Everyone was happy. Everyone but Sam, Lucy, and Antonio.

"Maybe Orson doesn't have anything to do with the school falling apart," Lucy said hopefully.

"No way!" Antonio exclaimed. "Nothing at Eerie Elementary is ever just a coincidence. Orson *always* has some crazy plan!"

"True," Sam said. "But what is his plan?"

Lucy and Antonio didn't reply.

Sam was only sure of one thing: The three of them needed to uncover Orson's plan before someone got hurt — *or worse!*

7
THE END OF ORSON?

The next morning, Sam, Lucy, and Antonio stepped onto school grounds.

"What on earth?" Antonio said.

"Who are all these people?" Lucy asked.

"And what are they doing to our school?" Sam said.

Construction workers in bright yellow hard hats were examining the building and taking measurements.

Trailers were set up across the soccer field. Principal Winik was directing students. "Find your teachers," he announced. "They will explain everything."

Sam and his friends spotted Ms. Grinker. They made their way through the crowd.

"Ms. Grinker, what is happening?" Lucy asked.

"Inside, inside," Ms. Grinker said. "I will explain."

Sam, Lucy, and Antonio entered a trailer. Their classmates were already seated.

The trailer was filled with desks and chairs. There was a whiteboard, but the walls were bare.

Ms. Grinker called for silence. Squeakers was inside her cage, running on her squeaky wheel.

"I realize everyone is curious to know what's going on outside," Ms. Grinker said. "Unfortunately, our beloved school is going to be torn down."

The entire class gasped.

"The building is too old," Ms. Grinker continued. "It has become a danger."

"Not to mention it's super creepy," Antonio whispered to Sam and Lucy.

"And *alive*," Lucy added.

"Class will be held here," Ms. Grinker continued, "until we have a new school building."

Sam raised his hand. "Ms. Grinker, when will the old building be torn down?"

"Tomorrow," Ms. Grinker said.

Ms. Grinker started class like usual. But Sam could not pay attention. He stared out the window, watching Eerie Elementary and thinking, *it feels like the school is watching me . . .*

Finally, it was time for recess. But the playground was overrun with construction workers, so recess was held on the soccer field.

Sam's friends were both overjoyed by Ms. Grinker's news about the school.

"Orson Eerie will be defeated at last! And *we're* not even the ones who are going to do it!" Antonio said. He looked like he was ready to run a victory lap around the school.

"We'll get a new, *not* monstrous school," Lucy said as she jumped up and down. "Won't that be nice?"

Sam smiled. But inside, he had doubts. If the school were destroyed, would Orson Eerie be destroyed, too? Sam wasn't so sure . . .

FROM BAD TO WORSE

8

Sam spotted Mr. Nekobi across the soccer field. He was talking to one of the construction workers.

"Look," Sam said to Lucy and Antonio. "Mr. Nekobi seems upset about something. Let's find out what it is."

The three friends hurried across the field. As they approached, the construction worker stomped away.

"What's wrong?" Sam asked. "What were you talking to that man about?"

Mr. Nekobi looked frightened. "Come," he said.

Sam, Antonio, and Lucy followed Mr. Nekobi back across the field. The old man sat down.

"That was the foreman — he's the head construction worker," Mr. Nekobi said. "I asked him what would be done with the remains of the school after it was torn down."

"What did he say?" Sam asked. Antonio and Lucy leaned forward.

"Some of the rubble will be sent to the junkyard," Mr. Nekobi said slowly. "But pieces of brick and metal will help repair other buildings in the town. Parts of Eerie Elementary will be reused . . ."

Sam's mind raced. *Does each brick contain some small part of Orson Eerie? Each nut, each bolt — could they all hold a piece of Orson Eerie's monstrous powers?*

"Could Orson Eerie's evil powers spread through town?" Sam asked.

Mr. Nekobi frowned. "I do not know. But that is what I fear . . ."

Just minutes earlier, Sam, Lucy, and Antonio had been celebrating. But now it seemed like they might be worse off than ever!

"We need more information about how Orson's powers would work in that situation," Lucy said.

"And we need it fast!" Antonio added.

Sam smiled. "I know just where to look!"

THE PLAN IS REVEALED

9

After school, Sam, Antonio, and Lucy ran to Jasper Eerie's house.

The house sat at the end of a cracked driveway. The roof was sunken in and the house was sort of crooked.

Lucy knocked on the door. It creaked open, and Jasper appeared. "Hello, kids," he said.

"No time for hellos!" Sam said as he rushed into the house.

This had been Orson Eerie's home — and it was full of his creepy, old things. Ancient trunks and boxes filled the kitchen. There were stacks of Orson Eerie's notebooks and journals on the table.

"What's going on?" Jasper asked.

"Eerie Elementary is about to be torn down!" Antonio said.

"That's good news!" Jasper said.

Sam said, "Maybe. Or it might be *the worst news*! Can we sit down?"

They gathered around the kitchen table. Jasper listened while the kids explained what had happened the past two days. They told Jasper they feared the school's evil powers could spread.

"That sounds like Orson all right," Jasper said.

"We need to know what will happen to Orson's power if pieces of the school are moved," Antonio said. "Like if they end up in other buildings."

Sam eyed the piles of Orson's work. "Well," he said, picking up a notebook. "I guess we should start reading."

It was almost dinner time, and they hadn't found *anything* useful.

Antonio chuckled as he read a document. "Check this out: Apparently Orson Eerie was super ticklish. He was researching a cure for ticklishness!"

"Weird," said Sam. "But not helpful."

Just then, Lucy discovered something that was helpful. She was flipping through a notebook when a piece of paper slipped out.

Sam picked it up. "It's a drawing of Eerie Elementary!" he said.

Lucy gasped when she saw what it said on top:

"Demolition . . . ," Jasper said curiously. "This means Orson planned for this. This drawing explains what will happen when the school is torn down."

"What are these arrows?" Antonio asked.

As Sam looked at the drawing, everything suddenly made *perfect* and *terrible* sense. "This drawing shows Orson Eerie's power spreading!" Sam said. "Orson *is* making the school fall apart!"

"The falling plaque and the crumbling walls . . . It was all Orson's doing," Antonio said. "We thought Orson would finally be defeated, but —"

"Instead, it's the opposite!" Lucy interrupted. "Orson's evil powers *will* spread across the town!"

Sam nodded. "He will be more powerful than ever before . . . Unless we can stop the demolition . . ."

There was a terrible quiet in the room.

Jasper Eerie broke the silence. "I will try to find out more, but I won't set foot on school grounds ever again. *You three* are the only hope of stopping this nightmare."

STOP!

10

The next day, Sam stared out the window during class. He saw construction workers hurrying about, removing boxes from the school. All day, it felt like Eerie Elementary was watching him.

Just as the school day was ending, Sam's desk began to shake. His sneakers bounced against the floor. The entire trailer was quaking!

Sam watched Squeakers hide beneath a pile of sawdust.

Lucy's and Antonio's eyes were wide.

But Sam realized that — for once — this was *not* Orson Eerie's doing. A massive truck rumbled past the window. The trailer shook harder, and a bulldozer followed.

"Oh no!" Sam whispered to his friends. "The demolition of Eerie Elementary is about to start."

Ms. Grinker dismissed the class and told everyone to head straight home. Sam and his classmates funneled outside. But no one headed home — they gathered on the field. It wasn't often that students got to watch their school be demolished in front of their eyes!

Sam saw a wrecking ball rumbling toward Eerie Elementary. The wrecking ball swung from a metal chain. The thick chain made a loud metallic creaking sound.

Sam caught Mr. Nekobi's eye from across the field. He was frowning.

In moments, the demolition would begin! All hope appeared to be lost . . .

But suddenly, Sam heard a familiar voice yelling, "STOP!"

Antonio was speeding toward the school, shouting at the top of his lungs: "STOP! STOP!"

Lucy grabbed Sam's sleeve. "What's Antonio doing?!"

"I'm not sure," Sam said. "But at least he's doing *something*! Come on!"

With that, Lucy and Sam raced after Antonio. Now they were *all* shouting:

ANTONIO'S QUICK THINKING

11

Sam, Lucy, and Antonio slid to a stop in front of the huge, swinging wrecking ball. Sam felt everyone — teachers, students, and construction workers — watching them.

Before Sam could ask what the plan was, Antonio shouted, "You can't knock down the school! Squeakers is inside!"

Sam's mind raced. *Squeakers is in her cage. I saw her before we left the trailer! What is Antonio thinking?*

The construction foreman climbed down from behind the controls. His yellow hard hat was shiny in the afternoon sun.

"*Who* or *what* is Squeakers?" the foreman asked, crossing his arms.

"Squeakers is our class pet!" Antonio said.

"She's a furry brown hamster," Lucy said. She looked up at the foreman with wide, puppy-dog eyes.

"Yeah, and I just saw her through that window!" Antonio said. "You *can't* knock down Eerie Elementary while Squeakers is inside!"

Principal Winik stomped across the field. He didn't look happy . . .

Sam swallowed. *Anyone can look inside Squeakers's cage! They'll know Antonio is lying!*

A moment later, Sam's classmate Bryan appeared in the trailer doorway. "It's true!" Bryan yelled. "Squeakers isn't in her cage!"

Sam's eyes widened.

Antonio flashed his friends a sneaky grin. "Look, guys," he whispered. Antonio opened his coat. Squeakers! The fur ball was peeking over the top of Antonio's shirt pocket. "I nabbed her from the cage while everyone was rushing outside."

"Smart!" Lucy said.

Antonio snapped his jacket shut before anyone else saw the hamster.

With a deep sigh, Principal Winik said, "All demolition must stop until we find — *ahem* — Squeakers."

A burst of applause came from the students and teachers. They were eager to watch the demolition — but no one wanted it to happen with a hamster inside!

The foreman's face was bright red. He stomped back to his construction crew and ordered them to search the school. Men and women in hard hats trudged inside to look for a missing hamster.

Just then, Sam noticed Principal Winik and the foreman disappear around the side of the school. "Guys, follow me," Sam whispered to Lucy and Antonio.

The friends crept around the building. They ducked down behind a dumpster. Sam cupped his hand to his ear.

"If you don't find the pet, continue with the demolition tomorrow at 7:00 a.m. sharp. We're tearing down Eerie Elementary," said Principal Winik. "No matter what."

TOWN SQUARE SCARES

12

"Antonio, your quick thinking bought us some time," said Sam.

Sam, Lucy, and Antonio were walking home from school. The air was cold. Antonio pulled his jacket tighter — but not *too tight*. Squeakers was still in his pocket.

"Yeah, but not a lot of time. We'll be in the *exact* same situation tomorrow," Antonio said. "The school will be knocked down!"

"We can't let that happen," Lucy said.

Sam's mind raced. This was Orson's most wicked plan yet — and he had no idea how to stop it!

The friends stopped in front of Sam's house.

"Everyone, think hard," Sam said. "We *have* to come up with a plan!"

Antonio gently patted his pocket. "I'll look after this fur ball. Who knows — maybe she'll give me an idea!"

"I'm going to the town hall," Lucy said. "Maybe I can find some helpful information about the school."

"Okay," Sam said. "Let's meet at school early tomorrow morning."

The three friends split up.

That night, Sam could barely eat his dinner. He was too nervous. "I'm going to go to bed early," he told his mom.

His mom smiled. "Of course, honey. I bet you're stressed with everything going on at school."

Sam thought to himself, *Mom, if you only knew the truth . . .*

Sam fell asleep the second his head hit the pillow. But before he knew it, he was up — and he was walking through Eerie's town square. It was the middle of the night. The streets were quiet. *Too* quiet.

The town was *different.* Sam had a twisted feeling in his stomach. It was the same feeling he got when the school was about to attack. But now, he had that feeling in downtown Eerie.

The town suddenly roared to monstrous life! The grocery store's doors slammed open and shut. They had become a chomping mouth!

Tall streetlamps bent down and reached for Sam. Sam dodged them!

Buildings swayed. The mailbox clanged and envelopes flew out.

A fire hydrant burst, spewing water. The water took the form of terrifying liquid tentacles!

Every bit of the town roared to life. The monstrous town of Eerie was behaving like the monstrous school, Eerie Elementary!

Stoplights turned completely red — and the red beams formed one giant spotlight. It shone directly on Sam!

Suddenly, everything went quiet.

Everything had gone back to normal. But only for a moment . . .

At the end of Main Street, two huge headlights flashed on. Sam was bathed in blinding white light.

It was the wrecking ball. It hung from a crane. The crane was atop a truck. And the truck was speeding toward Sam!

Sam stood frozen in the street.

The truck had changed. The headlights looked like narrow eyes. The bumper formed a thin mustache.

It was a face. It was the face of Orson Eerie.

NO TIME TO WASTE

13

Sam woke up. His pajamas were soaked in sweat. His heart was pounding.

"It was just a scary nightmare . . . ," Sam told himself.

But Sam knew the nightmare could come true — if he and his friends didn't stop the demolition of Eerie Elementary.

Sam couldn't go back to sleep. All he could picture was that terrifying face and the swinging wrecking ball. Just then, he realized something awful . . .

The wrecking ball is on school grounds. Orson Eerie can demolish the school himself! He doesn't need to wait for the construction workers to do it!

In a flash, Sam was up and dressed. He hurried downstairs and scribbled a quick note to his parents.

Sam ran to Lucy's house. He tossed a pebble at Lucy's window. The window lifted.

Lucy rubbed her eyes. "Sam?" she said. She was fighting off a yawn. "What are you doing here? It's still dark out."

"I had a nightmare!" Sam said. "Now I think Orson is going to use the wrecking ball to destroy the school all by himself!"

Moments later, Lucy came out of her front door.

Antonio's house was next. Lucy tapped his window with a branch.

Antonio's window rattled open. He could tell something important was happening. "Coming!" he said.

He slipped Squeakers into his front pocket as he ran outside.

"You're bringing Squeakers?" Lucy asked.

"I can't leave her," Antonio replied as he petted Squeakers. "I bonded with this cutie! She's the best. Aren't you, my little buddy?"

"Oh, Lucy!" Sam said. "I forgot to ask. Did you have any luck at the town hall?"

"Not really," Lucy said with a sigh. "I did bump into Jasper, though. I told him everything that happened yesterday. He said he'd keep searching for information."

"Okay, well . . . No time to waste!" Sam said. "Come on! I'm afraid the demolition is already starting!"

The friends began running.

It was almost dawn when they arrived at Eerie Elementary. A blue-gray fog hung over the school. It was a cold winter morning, and it felt even colder near the school. An icy chill ran down Sam's spine.

They hurried past the trailers, across the soccer field, and over to the playground. Eerie Elementary loomed over everything. It made Sam think of an abandoned castle. Everything was still. Then —

GRRRR-OOOM!

The sound of an engine cut through the early morning quiet.

Sam's nightmare was coming to life.

Bright headlights flooded the school. The truck rumbled. The crane began to move. The wrecking ball started swinging.

But there was no one inside the truck!

DANGER AT DAWN

14

The monstrous truck thundered toward Eerie Elementary. The wrecking ball began swinging faster and faster.

Sam had been right: Orson Eerie was going to destroy the school on his own!

The wrecking ball swung into the school, and — **WHAM!!!**

An entire school wall exploded! Chunks of brick rained down on the grass.

"We have to do something!" Lucy cried.

The rumbling truck engine was so loud it was deafening.

Sam stepped forward. He cupped his hands around his mouth and shouted, "Orson Eerie! Before you destroy that building, you've got three hall monitors to deal with!"

The wrecking ball slowed. The big truck turned toward the friends. Its engine barked.

Sam gulped.

This was *exactly* like his nightmare.

The truck seemed to have a face — and that face was looking straight at Sam. The headlights flashed from yellow to red. They were like angry, monstrous eyes. The engine snarled and growled.

"You got his attention," Antonio said, his voice trembling. "Now what?"

Suddenly, the truck sped toward them! The wrecking ball whipped through the air. Sam, Antonio, and Lucy ducked behind the jungle gym as the huge metal ball swung.

SMASH!

The friends scrambled out of the way as the jungle gym exploded into pieces. The sound of the cranking crane filled the air. The wrecking ball swung again.

"Watch out!" Sam cried.

TICKLE FIGHT!

15

There was a loud **CRUNCH** as the wrecking ball smashed into the swing set and ripped it from the ground.

Sam, Antonio, and Lucy dove behind the monkey bars. They could hear the wrecking ball slicing through the air.

Suddenly, Antonio started laughing.

"What's so funny?" Lucy exclaimed. "This is no time for laughing! Orson is trying to bash us!"

"I — I — I don't mean to!" Antonio said. He was laughing so hard that he could barely speak. "It's Squeakers! She crawled up my shirt! Her feet tickle!"

Squeakers darted out through Antonio's collar. She scampered into his lap. Antonio scooped her up and caught his breath.

"Wait a second," Sam said. "Didn't we read that —"

Lucy finished Sam's thought. "Orson was terribly ticklish! Maybe Squeakers can help us again!" she said.

In a flash, Antonio was racing toward the truck. The wrecking ball swung over his head as he set Squeakers down in the grass. Squeakers scrambled atop the truck.

Antonio stepped back. Squeakers was darting in and out of the truck, around the crane, and scampering along the roof.

The engine let out a howling, high-pitched squeal. Sam realized it sounded like *laughter. The truck is giggling!*

"It's working!" Lucy said.

"Squeakers is tickling Orson Eerie — and I bet she doesn't even know it!" Sam exclaimed.

The wrecking ball swung wildly. The engine let out more loud, terrifying, crazed laughter. And then —

CLINK. CLINK. CLINK.

The wrecking ball was lifted high into the air. The crane swung, and the ball was directly above the truck.

"Orson is going to use the wrecking ball on Squeakers!" Lucy shouted.

"No!" Antonio cried. "My little buddy will be smashed!"

"This truck has done enough damage to the school," Sam said. "It's time for it to damage *itself*! But first, I'll save Squeakers!"

"It's too dangerous!" Lucy exclaimed.

Sam raced forward. He leapt past the broken playground equipment. He bounded onto the truck. The cold metal chilled him to his core.

"Get down from there!" Antonio called out.

But Sam knew this was their one chance to defeat the wrecking ball. "Squeakers! Come here!" Sam said. He reached across the roof for the speeding hamster.

"The ball is about to drop!" Antonio cried.

Sam looked up. He saw the huge metal ball above him.

Suddenly, Sam began giggling. Squeakers had darted up his jacket sleeve. An instant later, the tiny hamster's face poked out. Sam grabbed her.

And just in time.

"Gotcha!" Sam said. Sam tucked his hands over his chest and dove onto the damp grass.

Antonio and Lucy ran over. They dragged Sam away from the monstrous truck, just as —

The massive wrecking ball smashed down! It was the loudest sound Sam had ever heard. Metal exploded. Electrical sparks shot out. The ball plunged *through* the truck.

Sam stood up and Squeakers leapt into Antonio's hands. The three friends looked at the rubble. The sun was rising higher in the sky.

"Nice job, Sam! The monstrous truck destroyed itself!" Antonio said.

"But what about the rest of Orson's plan?" Lucy asked. "The construction crew could show up any second!"

Sam pointed. "They're already here . . ."

NOT OVER YET . . .

16

Sam, Antonio, and Lucy watched the construction crew march across the soccer field. The foreman led the way. Mr. Nekobi and Principal Winik hurried behind him.

Lucy gulped. "How do we explain the truck?" she asked.

It was a jumble of bent metal. Clouds of smoke poured from the engine.

"We can't explain it," Antonio said. "I vote we run behind the building! Then we'll come walking around. We'll whistle, too. Whistling *always* makes you look innocent!"

But Sam knew it was too late for that.

The foreman looked *furious*. "My truck! My wrecking ball!" he exclaimed. He glared at Sam, Antonio, and Lucy. "I know you had something to do with this! Admit it!"

Antonio smiled and said, "Sir, do you *really* think we could have done this?"

"We don't know how to use a wrecking ball," Lucy said.

"Yeah! We're just a bunch of third-grade hall monitors," Sam said.

"Maybe it was a malfunction," Mr. Nekobi said. "Perhaps your workers didn't properly shut it down yesterday."

The foreman glared at Mr. Nekobi.

Principal Winik stepped between them. "Regardless," he said. "We're just lucky no one was hurt."

The foreman was so angry he was almost shaking. "I'll have another truck here this afternoon," he said. "The wrecking ball will swing!"

Oh no! Sam thought. *We only stopped part of Orson Eerie's plan — we didn't totally defeat him!*

"And I see the class pet has been found, so there's no reason to delay," Principal Winik said, glancing at Squeakers. "This school will be torn down today."

Suddenly, a voice called out, "No, it won't!"

Sam spun around.

It was Jasper Eerie. He was standing outside the school gate.

Jasper was waving a piece of paper. Lucy sprinted across the lawn and grabbed it. Her eyes skimmed it over.

A moment later, she came hurrying back. She waved the document.

"This is from the town hall!" Lucy said, smiling. "It says that Eerie Elementary is a historical landmark. If you demolish it, you'll be breaking the law. This building can *never* be torn down!"

Principal Winik read the paper. He sighed. "It's true. This means the building must be repaired. Brick by brick."

Suddenly, the school doors blew open. A great wailing sound — like a scream — came from deep inside Eerie Elementary.

Principal Winik, Mr. Nekobi, and the foreman all looked at the school. "Wha– what was that sound?" the foreman asked. His voice trembled.

"Just the old heating system," Mr. Nekobi said quickly. "It makes the oddest sounds."

But Sam knew it was the pained howling of Orson Eerie. The new information had stopped Orson's evil plan!

Soon, the construction workers were hard at work — but they weren't tearing the school down. They were putting it back together. They were repairing the gym and patching the walls and fixing the playground.

Sam, Lucy, and Antonio walked to the trailer for class.

"So we *defeated* Eerie Elementary by *saving* Eerie Elementary," Sam said. "Weird."

Antonio nodded. "Super weird! But it's good because school will go back to normal!"

"But it's also bad," Lucy said. "Because — well — *school will be back to normal*!"

"A hall monitor's work is never done," Antonio said.

Sam nodded. "That's for sure. Not at Eerie Elementary . . ."

Shhhh!

This news is top secret: **Jack Chabert** is a pen name for *New York Times* bestselling author Max Brallier. (Max uses a made-up name instead of his real name so Orson Eerie won't come after him, too!)

Max was once a hall monitor at Joshua Eaton Elementary School in Reading, MA. But today, Max lives in a super-weird, old apartment building in New York City. His days are spent writing, playing video games, and reading comic books. And at night, he walks the halls, always prepared for the moment when his building will come alive.

Max is the author of more than twenty books for children, including the middle-grade series The Last Kids on Earth and Galactic Hot Dogs. Visit the author at www.MaxBrallier.com.

Matt Loveridge loves illustrating children's books. When he's not painting or drawing, he likes hiking, biking, and drinking milk from the carton. He lives in the mountains of Utah with his wife and kids, and their black dog named Blue.

HOW MUCH DO YOU KNOW ABOUT

Eerie Elementary

Classes Are CANCELED?

Why is Mr. Nekobi worried about reusing pieces of the school? What proof do Sam and his friends find that confirms he is right?

Squeakers plays an important part in the fight against Orson Eerie — twice! Explain.

Look at page 81. What is happening in the picture?

How does Jasper help the hall monitors in the end?

Draw a comic strip (using both words and pictures) to recount how the hall monitors stop the school building from being torn down.